Diamond Fairy Tales

GEM CLASSICS LIBRARY

Retold by Jane Carruth

RAND McNALLY & COMPANY

Chicago • New York • San Francisco

Contents

Hansel and Gretel

THERE WAS once a poor woodcutter who was blessed with two loving children – a boy called Hansel and a girl called Gretel. When their own dear mother died, the woodcutter married again and this time he chose a wife who was neither loving nor gentle.

The woodcutter worked hard but soon he found he could no longer sell his wood in the market. Worse still, his savings were dwindling.

"What shall we do, wife?" he groaned, as they faced each other over the kitchen table. "My savings are gone and there is scarcely enough food in the house to feed you and the children."

"Then we must rid ourselves of the children," said his wife, after no more than a moment's thought. "Without them we could manage quite well. Why, Hansel eats as much as you do."

The woodcutter could scarcely believe his ears when he heard this, but his wife was determined. She nagged and scolded him, and in the evening, when Hansel and Gretel had gone upstairs to bed, she began all over again.

"You must take them into the forest early in the morning and leave them there," she said. "It's the only sensible thing to do. I am not willing to starve on their account."

In vain, her husband told her that he loved his children and that he would rather die than do them harm. His wife refused to listen and became so angry that her voice got louder and louder. The noise of the shouting woke Hansel, so he climbed out of bed and tip-toed to the top of the stairs. As he stood there, quiet as a mouse, he heard his stepmother say, "Then it's settled. Tomorrow we take them into the forest and leave them there."

Hansel crept back to his little bed and lay there, wide awake, until at last Gretel crept in beside him. "I'm so hungry," she whispered, "I can't sleep, and besides I thought I heard our stepmother shouting."

Then Hansel told her what their fate was to be in the morning. "But take heart, little sister," he went on. "I've thought up a plan already.

As soon as the house is quiet, I'm going down into the garden to fill my pockets with shining white pebbles."

The moon was shining so brightly that the pebbles looked like real silver pennies as Hansel bent down and picked them up. He stuffed his pockets until they were bulging. Then he went back indoors and closed the back door gently behind him, before running upstairs to Gretel.

"Now we have nothing to be afraid of," he told her, showing her some of the pebbles. "But don't say a word about them when we set off tomorrow for the forest."

Early the next morning, so early that the sun was not yet up, Hansel and Gretel heard their stepmother's harsh voice telling them to hurry and get dressed. "We're taking you into the forest, today," she shouted. "So don't play about but get ready quickly."

There was nothing but stale crusts to eat for breakfast so the meal was quickly over. Then their stepmother gave Hansel and Gretel a slice of stale bread. "Don't eat it now. Keep it for your dinner," she warned them. "There will be nothing else."

As they set out, Hansel lingered behind, fingering the pebbles in his pocket and hoping that he could drop them, one by one, without being seen.

"Why do you walk so slowly?" his father called over his shoulder after they had gone some way into the forest.

"I keep turning around to see if I can catch sight of my little white cat on the roof," Hansel told him.

"What a fool you are!" snapped his stepmother. "Your white cat is more likely to be busy catching mice. Hurry up, if you don't want a slap."

When they reached the middle of the forest where the trees grew so close together that they blotted out the sun, their father told them to rest. "Your mother and I will gather as many sticks as we can," he said, giving Gretel a sad look. "But first I will make a fire for you while we are away so that you won't be cold."

Hansel and Gretel sat close together beside the fire, hoping against hope that their father would return. For a time they could hear the sound of his axe as he struck the trees. Then a silence fell upon the forest; even the little birds no longer sang.

"How dark it grows," said Gretel at last. "Oh, how frightened I am! They are not coming back for us, I am sure of it now."

Hansel put his arm around his sister's shoulder, as he said, "It is too

9

dark now to follow my trail of pebbles. Let's try and get some sleep. Don't be afraid, Gretel. I'll take care of you."

Gretel closed her eyes, snuggling up close to her brother, and Hansel kept watch until at last the dark night sky was lit by the silvery light from the moon. "Come," he whispered softly to his sister, "it's time to go. I shall be able to find the pebbles easily now with the help of the friendly moon."

Hand in hand, the children set out and Hansel pointed out the pebbles as they walked along. "If we hurry," he said, "we shall be home by morning."

By early morning, Hansel and Gretel reached their cottage and oh, how happy they were to see their father again. And how happy he was too. He hugged and kissed them and vowed that never again would they be parted.

But his wife was not at all pleased to see the children. She scowled and turned away from them and the poor woodcutter knew it would not be long before she tried once again to lose them in the forest. How right he was!

One night, just a few days after their return, his wife said, "Nothing has changed. There is not enough food in the cupboard to feed a sparrow. We must take them into the forest early tomorrow morning and this time make certain that they do not find their way home."

Once again, the woodcutter pleaded and argued and once again the wife began to shout. And, as soon as the house was quiet, Hansel stole down the stairs.

"I will fill my pockets with shining white pebbles once more," he

told himself, as he reached the back door. "Then we will be saved again."

Alas, when Hansel tried to open the back door, he found it locked and the key missing. What could he do now? Safely back in bed, he thought and thought. At last, he made up his mind to use the bread his stepmother was sure to give him. "I'll lay a trail of breadcrumbs," he finally decided, before his eyes closed in sleep. "The crumbs will be just as good as the pebbles."

But, oh dear me, how wrong Hansel was! The next morning as they trudged further and further into the forest, Hansel dropped his crumbs. Can you guess what happened? All the little birds of the forest flew down from the trees and feasted on the bread!

Gretel began to cry bitterly when, once again, they found themselves all alone in the deep dark forest. "Don't cry, little sister," said Hansel. "My trail of breadcrumbs will help us to find our way home."

But as the moon lit the forest he discovered the awful truth. Not a single crumb could he find. But he was so brave that he smiled and whistled and pretended that he knew the way home even without the help of the breadcrumbs.

"I – I d–don't think we shall ever find our way h–home," Gretel sobbed, as Hansel took her hand. "We'll be eaten by wolves."

"It's too dark now to find the right path," Hansel told her. "Let's sleep a little as we did before and then start out. You're safe with me so don't cry."

Have you ever been lost in a big forest? Have you ever run along paths that lead nowhere and fallen into ditches and tripped over trailing branches? Have you ever been so frightened that you couldn't make your tired legs carry you another step?

It was just like that with Gretel after walking and running and walking again for nearly a whole day. She was so scared that at last she sat down and said she couldn't take another step. Hansel was tired and frightened too but being a boy he couldn't let his sister see his despair. "We must keep walking," he said at last. "We're sure to find the right path soon."

As he spoke, he suddenly saw on the branch of a tree just ahead of them a most beautiful white bird. It was like no other bird he had ever seen and he pointed to it. Gretel dried her eyes and stared at the bird.

"How pretty it is," she said. "Like a white dove but nicer." As she got up and ran towards it the bird flew to another tree a short distance away and once again perched motionless on a branch.

"It's just as if the bird wanted us to follow it," said Hansel. "Shall we, Gretel? Perhaps it will take us safely out of the forest."

Hand in hand, the children ran after the pretty white bird and soon they found themselves in a clearing in the forest and staring at the strangest little cottage you could ever imagine. The snow-white bird flew down and sat on the roof while Hansel and Gretel walked towards the cottage.

"Look!" Gretel cried, clapping her hands, "the walls are made of bread and covered with cakes."

"And the windows are made of clear sugar," exclaimed Hansel. "And the roof has tiles made of biscuits!"

"Oh, I'm so hungry," whispered Gretel. "Do – do you think we could have a tiny nibble?"

For answer, Hansel reached up and broke off a piece of roof and ther Gretel began to eat some of the window. "It tastes just like barley sugar," she laughed. "I don't feel frightened any more."

Hansel had eaten quite a big part of the roof when suddenly the door opened, and a woman, all bent and wrinkled and old as old can be, hobbled out of the cottage on two crutches. At the sight of her, Gretel screamed and dropped her sugar windowpane, and Hansel said, "Begging your pardon, ma'am, we meant no harm."

The old woman smiled and nodded. "How glad I am to see you, dear children," she said, in a croaky kind of voice. "Do come in and stay with me. I will take care of you." And she took them both by the hand and led them inside.

"She looks like a witch," Gretel whispered to her brother, "but she can't be, she is so kind. Just look what she is giving us to eat."

The old woman busied herself setting out pancakes and honey on the table. And this was followed by sugar cookies and apples and nuts.

"Eat all you can," she said, as she hobbled back and forth between the kitchen and the front room. "And drink your milk. Milk helps you to grow big and strong."

What a feast the children had and, afterwards, the old woman took them into another room and showed them two little beds covered with flowery sheets.

"There is where you will sleep," she croaked. "And in the morning I will show you some toys you can play with."

Now the old woman was really and truly a wicked witch. Her snow-white bird was trained to fly out into the forest and search for lost children and bring them to her. And whenever children fell into her power she fed them up to make them round and fat and then roasted them in her big oven.

If Hansel and Gretel had known anything about witches they would have looked at her red eyes and known her for what she was. But of course they had never before met a witch so they did not know.

Early the next morning, however, they learned the truth. As soon as they were dressed, the witch seized Hansel and carried him outside.

"In you go," she cackled, thrusting him into a big cage. "When you are nice and plump I will eat you for my dinner."

Then she went back to Gretel. "Fetch the water from the well," she commanded. "Move yourself, you lazy child. From now on you will be my servant. And when I have eaten your brother I will fatten you up and eat you."

Of course poor Gretel burst into tears and begged for her brother's life but the wicked witch only laughed and drove her out of the house, telling her to make haste and fetch the water.

For the next few days the witch busied herself with her cooking. Apple pies smothered in cream were taken out to Hansel every hour and often there was chicken and baked potatoes and jam doughnuts. But for Gretel there was nothing but stale crusts of bread and cups of water to drink.

At the end of a week, the witch went to Hansel's cage and cried, "Hansel, Hansel, stretch out your finger so that I may feel if you grow fat!"

You may well wonder why the witch had to feel Hansel's finger but the truth is that witches cannot see very well.

Now Hansel was not only brave but clever. Instead of giving the witch his finger to feel, he thrust out a chicken bone.

"I cannot understand it," the witch grumbled after two weeks. "You eat everything I give you yet you grow no fatter." And so angry was she that she pushed Gretel into a corner of the kitchen and refused even to feed her on scraps.

At the end of a month the witch vowed she would wait no longer. "I will eat that brother of yours today," she cried. "Be he fat or thin he will be baked in my oven." And she told Gretel to fetch water while she lit the oven.

When Gretel returned, the witch said, "I have lit the oven but I cannot tell whether or not it is hot enough. Creep inside and see if it is properly heated."

But Gretel guessed that she meant to trap her in the oven and bake her first, so she said, "I – I do not know how to get in. Won't you show me?"

"What a stupid girl you are!" exclaimed the witch, impatiently. "The door is big enough. Watch me! I'll show you." And she opened the heavy door and put her head inside the oven.

Gretel knew what she must do. Suddenly brave, she crept up behind the witch and, with a great push, sent her toppling into the oven. Then she slammed shut the heavy door. And that was the end of the terrible witch, for there was no way out of the oven and she had no powers that would save her from being baked.

With a shout of joy, Gretel ran outside to the cage where her brother was a prisoner and set him free. Then together they ran back to the house. "I have seen where she keeps her treasure," said Gretel. "She has boxes filled with pearls and rubies and diamonds. Do you think we could take some back to our father?"

"Witches' treasure belongs to the one who finds it," said Hansel wisely. "So let us help ourselves."

Then Gretel showed him where the witch had hidden her treasure under the floorboards and Hansel filled his pockets with precious stones and then Gretel filled the pockets of her little apron. When they could carry no more, they ran out into the forest.

After walking for at least two hours, they came at last to a stretch of water. "What shall we do now?" Gretel asked. "Hansel, what shall we do? We cannot swim across this water and there is no boat."

Hansel sat down to think and Gretel looked all about her. Presently a white duck came swimming over the water and she cried,

"Little duck, little duck, can you see,
Hansel and Gretel waiting for thee?
There's not a boat, or a bridge in sight,
Take us across on your back so white."

To her joy, the duck swam over to them and Hansel sprang to his feet. "Do you think she will take us?" he asked.

"I know she will," said Gretel happily. "But we shall be too heavy for her if we both ride on her back. I will go first and then tell her to return for you."

So the good little duck carried first Gretel and then Hansel across the broad lake and when they were safely on the other side, Hansel said he was sure he could find his way home from there.

Soon they came upon the path which led them straight to their father's house and, in a few moments, they saw it among the trees. Gretel began to run and Hansel followed her, shouting with joy. As they burst into the kitchen, their father looked up from the table where he so often sat with his head in his hands, thinking about his long-lost children.

At first, he thought it was a dream but Gretel's warm arms were soon about his neck and Hansel was emptying his pockets on the table to show him the rubies and diamonds and pearls that would make them rich.

"Your stepmother is dead," the woodcutter said, at last. "And I am all alone. Day after day I have spent in sadness thinking that you were both lost to me forever."

Then Hansel told his father the whole story, from beginning to end, and the woodcutter said, "I care nothing for the precious stones. All I care about is that I have my beloved children safely back home. Now we shall be happy for always."

And they were, too. And there was always bread and meat in the cupboard for, after the woodcutter had sold the precious stones, there was enough money to buy everything they needed for the rest of their lives.

The Fairies

THERE ONCE lived a very bad-tempered and disagreeable widow who had two daughters. The elder, called Fanchon, had the same bad temper as her mother and was both spiteful and lazy, as well. She was especially spiteful to her sister, Rose, who had such a sweet temper and gentle nature that people wondered how they could be sisters.

Well, the widow favored her elder daughter. Besides being similar in temperament, Fanchon had another desire that her mother had – and that was to be a grand lady. The widow was not rich but whatever money she had, she spent on Fanchon. She had the best of everything and was so spoiled by her mother that she did no work at all in the house.

Rose, on the other hand, was treated like a servant. She wore her sister's cast-off dresses, cleaned the grates, scrubbed the floors and each morning trudged a mile or so to the village well to draw water. But no matter how hard she worked, she remained gentle and kind.

Early one morning, Rose set out with her pitcher as usual. When she reached the well, she was surprised to find an old woman there. Rose saw how bent her shoulders were and how tattered her shawl and she gave her a sweet smile as she set about filling her pitcher.

"Will you give me a drink of water from your pitcher?" asked the old woman, when Rose's task was done.

"Of course I will," said Rose. "You can have all the water you want. Sit down, madam, rest awhile and drink your fill."

Now the old woman was really a fairy in disguise. So many reports of Rose's kindness had reached her ears that she had come to see for herself if they were true.

After she had drunk the water, the fairy said, "You are as kind and gentle as people say you are. I have not been disappointed. Now I would like to bestow a gift upon you."

Rose, of course, had no idea that it was a fairy speaking and she said quickly, "I want nothing from you, dear lady. No, no, please do not try to give me anything. All I did was a simple kindness."

"And for that simple kindness," said the fairy, "I mean to give you a precious gift. Whenever you open your mouth to speak, flowers and jewels will fall from your lips."

Smiling, Rose picked up her pitcher and returned home, thinking that the poor old woman could not have possibly meant what she said. Her mother was waiting for her at the bottom of the garden. "You lazy good-for-nothing!" she screamed, when she saw Rose. "You've been gossiping, I'll be bound. The fire's out and your sister is waiting for you to clean her shoes . . ."

"I'm sorry, but I met . . ." Rose began and then stopped as sweet-smelling flowers and a shower of rubies dropped from her lips on to the ground at her feet.

Her mother bent down and picked up the rubies only, for the beautiful flowers meant nothing to her. Rose watched her, too astonished to speak, although she remembered clearly what the old woman had said.

"These rubies are real!" cried the widow. "What's all this?" And changing her mind about dealing Rose a slap, she took her arm instead and rushed her into the house.

There Rose began to tell of her meeting with the poor old woman at the well. As she spoke, flowers and precious stones dropped from her lips until every inch of the kitchen table glinted and sparkled.

"You're bewitched, child!" cried her mother, beside herself with

envy and greed as she saw the rubies and diamonds and precious gems. "Why should such good fortune happen to you? Now if only it had happened instead to my dear Fanchon!" And she shouted loudly for her unpleasant daughter to come into the kitchen.

When Fanchon saw the jewels and heard the story, she pinched Rose cruelly and hard out of jealousy and her mother said, "We must think what to do so that you can win a similar gift for yourself."

"Just as long as you don't expect me to walk a mile to the well," said Fanchon. "Such a walk over rough ground would ruin my slippers."

"But that is just what you must do!" cried her mother at last. "To-morrow morning you must take the pitcher to the well. If you see that old woman with the bent shoulders and shawl do anything she asks. Then she'll reward you in the same way as she has rewarded that sister of yours."

The next morning, with her mother's help, Fanchon managed to rise early. "What a nuisance," the girl grumbled, as her mother helped her into one of her prettiest dresses. "You know how I hate walking."

"Never mind," said her mother. "Think of the reward."

"There's one thing, though," said Fanchon when she was ready. "I'm not going to carry that common-looking pitcher that Rose takes. I'll take the silver flagon, then people will know I'm not a servant."

There was an ugly scowl on Fanchon's face when she reached the well. Her slippers were pinching her and the silver flagon had proved heavy to carry. Besides, she was so lazy that any kind of exercise increased her bad temper. To make matters worse there was no sign of the old woman her mother had said would be there. Instead, standing by the well, was a tall handsome lady, richly dressed and with an air of command about her.

Fanchon stared at her rudely and the lady smiled and said, "When you have filled your flagon from the well, will you give me a drink?"

"I will not!" retorted Fanchon. "Why should I? You look as if you could afford servants. I'm not your servant. If you want a drink, get it yourself."

Now the richly dressed lady was really the fairy who had spoken to Rose, though, of course, Fanchon had no way of knowing this.

"You are not very polite," said the fairy, as Fanchon turned away from her.

"What I am has nothing to do with you," said Fanchon over her shoulder. "So mind your own business."

"Such bad manners," said the fairy, "deserve one of my more special gifts. With every word you speak, toads and vipers will drop from your lips."

Fanchon paid very little attention to her words. Certain now that the old woman was not going to appear, she set off for home without even filling her flagon with water. As soon as she was within sight of her house, her mother came running down the road to greet her.

"Well?" she gasped, all out of breath and trembling with excitement. "Did you see her? Did she reward you for your kindness?"

"She wasn't there . . ." Fanchon replied angrily, and then stopped, for out of her mouth had dropped three fat toads and three wriggling snakes.

"It's all the fault of that sister of yours," stormed the widow, when Fanchon was inside the house. "No, no, don't say another word," she added quickly, for already the floor was covered with toads and vipers as Fanchon poured out her story. "Just wait till I lay my hands on her."

But when the angry widow began searching the house for her daughter, Rose was nowhere to be found. She had heard and seen all that had happened to Fanchon and she knew that her mother would put all the blame on her and beat her cruelly. Trembling with fear, she put her few belongings into a little bag and fled into the forest.

Too frightened to return home, Rose wandered about the forest

for the rest of the day and then, as darkness began to fall, lay down under a tree. So unhappy was she by now that she could not stop herself from beginning to cry.

Her gentle weeping disturbed the little birds and they flew down to try and comfort her. But for once Rose could take no pleasure in their soft pretty feathers. She sobbed the louder and the sound of her weeping caught the ear of the king's son as he rode homewards after a day's hunting.

His astonishment was great when he came upon the beautiful girl alone in the forest. "Who are you? Where do you come from?" asked the Prince, as he came up to her. "I have never seen you before."

"That is not likely, sire," Rose began, smiling in spite of her sadness. As she spoke, rubies and flowers fell from her lips on to the grass. She stopped immediately but the Prince, recovering from his surprise, begged her to tell him her story.

Well, by the end of it, the Prince was more than half in love with Rose. He had long been searching for a girl as kind and gentle as Rose and to find one whose every word produced a precious stone was wonderful indeed. He took her back to his palace and by the end of the week had made her his Princess.

The news of her sister's good fortune soon reached Fanchon. For very good reason she had spoken very little since the day she visited the well. But now she could not contain herself and toads and vipers hopped and crawled all over the kitchen as she raged on and on.

At last her mother could bear it no longer and she drove the miserable girl from the house, saying it would be best for both of them if Fanchon lived alone for then she would be able to hold her tongue. She was right, of course, and from that day onwards, the proud, spiteful Fanchon lived all by herself in a hut on the edge of the forest and never once did she dare to open her mouth again.

The Proud Beetle

ONCE UPON a time there lived an Emperor. Now this Emperor had a very favorite horse. He was indeed a very noble creature with big bright eyes and a mane that hung over his neck like a veil. He had served his master well in battle and more than once had helped to save his life in the thick of the fighting. To show his affection and appreciation the Emperor had had shoes of pure gold put on the horse's feet.

Now all this and much more the horse had many times explained to a large black Beetle that shared his royal stable.

"I don't care what you say," the Beetle remarked finally. "I share your stable and I should have golden shoes just like you." And, with that, he went to the blacksmith to ask for them.

"Don't you know why the Emperor's horse is given golden shoes?" asked the smith.

"I suppose I do," said the Beetle. "But I consider myself as good as the horse." And he stretched out his six thin legs.

"Be off with you," cried the blacksmith. "Away! Shoo!"

The Beetle flew around his head, saying, "Very well, I'll leave the stable forever and find a place where I shall be honored as one who knows the Emperor."

After flying a short while, the Beetle presently found himself in a beautiful flower garden, filled with the scent of roses and lavender.

"Welcome to our garden," said a dainty little ladybird. "It is very pretty here," and she turned around so that the Beetle could admire her red and black spotted coat.

"Do you think so?" exclaimed the Beetle. "I am used to a much better place than this!" And he flew on.

After a little while he came upon a caterpillar crawling along under the shadow of a huge cabbage leaf.

"Well, hello!" said the caterpillar, as the Beetle flew down to look at him. "Have you come to stay? It's really delightful here and very sheltered. If you stay long enough you'll have the pleasure of seeing me turn into a butterfly."

"I don't want to see anything of the kind," said the Beetle rudely. "I'll have you know that I have come out of the Emperor's stable and his favorite horse has to wear my golden shoes when I have finished with them," the Beetle lied. "Really, I don't know why I waste time talking to a common caterpillar." And away he flew.

Soon afterwards, the Beetle dropped down to the grass and, tired after so much exercise, he fell fast asleep. As he slept it began to rain. The heavy shower not only soaked his wings but sent him tumbling over and over in the wet grass. Goodness knows what would have become of the proud Beetle if he had not managed to find his six feet again. When he did, he rubbed the water out of his eyes and crawled into the sheltering folds of a linen sheet that had blown on to the ground. Very much out of temper, he lay perfectly still until the rain stopped.

When, at last, he felt strong enough to start his journey again, he found two frogs sitting close together on top of the sheet, their bright eyes shining with pleasure. "Wonderful weather this!" one of them said to the Beetle. "All this rain is so good for our skins. We love it!"

"I hate it," said the Beetle disagreeably. "In my royal stable at home it is warm and comfortable and not the least bit damp. The Emperor sees to everything. Did you know that his favorite horse has to wear my cast-off golden shoes?"

The frogs let out a few stupid croaks at this and the Beetle, certain that they were laughing at him, flew off in an angry way. "I must find a really snug dung-heap," he told himself, "where I can rest for a while." But although he flew around the garden once or twice he could not find a likely dung-heap. Instead, he came upon a ditch that the palace

gardeners had recently dug and there, sitting on the rich brown mud, were several other beetles.

"We are very happy and content here," they told him, as he flew down to join them. "It is true it is not quite as good as a dung-heap, but we mustn't complain."

"I come from the Emperor's stable," boasted the Beetle. "I was born there with golden shoes on my feet. I don't wear them now because I am on a secret mission for the Emperor."

The Beetle spoke with such pride and looked so important that the mother of three young girl beetles hurriedly pushed them forward so that the Beetle would notice them. "If you are thinking of settling down," she said, "I have three fine daughters still unmarried."

"They are certainly very pretty and quite as good-looking as the females in the stables," admitted the Beetle, looking at the youngest.

"Then you will take one of them for your wife?" asked the mother beetle hopefully. "The wedding can be arranged very quickly."

"I will," said the Beetle. "I'll take your youngest. One day she can come back with me to the stable on a visit and I'll show her off to the Emperor's favorite horse."

So the Beetle got married and for a little while was content. However, he soon began to find that as a husband he was expected to perform a number of humble tasks. This was too much for his pride and, by the end of the week, he left the ditch when his young wife was busy talking to her mother, and never went back.

By a great stroke of good fortune, the Beetle came, almost immediately, upon one of the Emperor's hothouses and finding the window open, flew inside. Here he felt immediately at home and settled down in the dark warm earth of one of the hot beds. Almost at once he fell fast asleep, and he dreamed that he was wearing the golden shoes that had once belonged to the Emperor's favorite horse. Most of his dream, however, was taken up with his search for two more golden shoes for, of course, the horse had need of only four while he required six.

When the Beetle awoke he began crawling about in the earth, thinking what a wonderful place the hothouse was and how presently he would sample some of the big-leafed plants that were everywhere. Suddenly, and to his great alarm, a hand seized him and rolled him over. The Beetle's six legs waved in the air and the little boy who had found him laughed aloud. He was the gardener's son and he liked the hothouse as much as the Beetle did.

"Look what we have here," he said to his friend, who had followed him inside. "A beetle – a big, fat black shining beetle. Let's have some fun with him."

"Don't hurt him!" said his friend, who was a sensible boy.

"Of course not," said the gardener's son. "We'll just send him on a journey."

"That suits me very well," thought the Beetle, when he heard this. "It will save me the bother of flying."

The boys ran down to the lake and put the Beetle in an old broken wooden shoe. They used a thin stick for a mast and bound the Beetle to it with woolen thread.

"Now I'm a sailor," the Beetle told himself proudly, as the boat floated away over the water. "What a story I'll have to tell that horse when I choose to visit him."

But the boys did not mean the Beetle to sail away out of their lives. Laughing and shouting they waded into the lake and brought the boat back to shore so that they could send it out again on a different course. If you think this was cruel you are perfectly correct and soon the gardener's boy grew quite ashamed of himself. He bent down to set the Beetle free and tumbled into the water. Now the boy was in trouble himself and likely enough to get a beating from his father. His friend said, "It serves you right!" And he ran off.

Meanwhile, the boat was drifting away into the middle of the lake and the Beetle was just beginning to wonder what could be the end of his adventure, when a dragonfly came whirring over his head.

"Beautiful weather," said the dragonfly. "I'll rest here for a minute and enjoy the sunshine. Are you having a nice time?"

"I don't think I am," said the Beetle. "I'm not exactly free to fly away when it suits me."

"Well, I am!" said the dragonfly, and off he went.

"The world does not deserve me," the Beetle told himself, as he watched the dragonfly go. "I come from the Emperor's stable and I am given no honor. Well, I have my pride. I will not be content until the world accepts me for what I am."

The old wooden shoe drifted on and on, over the lake until the Beetle began to wonder at last what was to become of him. "Perhaps it is all over for me," he thought. "If I had been given my golden shoes in the first place I would have stayed in the stable and been equal to that horse."

But it was not over for the Beetle. Two girls were rowing on the lake. They saw the Beetle's boat and they saw the Beetle.

"Look at that old wooden shoe sailing along," said one.

"And the little beetle bound to its mast," said the other. "Let's row over and set the Beetle free."

One of the girls had a small pair of scissors in her pocket and with these she cut the woolen thread that kept the Beetle prisoner. Picking him up, she held him gently in her hand while her friend rowed ashore. Once there, they set the Beetle free. Up, up he flew and then down through the open door of a long, low, building. Can you guess where he landed? He was back in the stable and clinging to the beautiful mane of the Emperor's favorite horse.

"Now, is this not very extraordinary?" the Beetle cried, when he felt stronger. "Here I am sitting on the Emperor's horse just like the Emperor himself! It is quite clear to me now why the horse was given his golden shoes. He is wearing them in my honor. I am equal to the Emperor in importance."

And with a deep sigh of happiness, he closed his eyes in well-earned sleep.

The Witch in the Woods

THERE WAS once a poor orphan girl called Gertha who worked as a servant to a very rich family. Gertha was gentle and kind and the family liked her so much that whenever they went on vacation they took her with them.

One holiday, the family decided to go for a long trip through the mountains. They were enjoying themselves very much and all went well until they came to a lonely stretch of road with woods on either side. Suddenly, a band of fierce robbers sprang from the trees and before anyone knew what was happening, the robber chief cut free the horses, upturned the carriage and killed Gertha's master and mistress. Trembling with fright, Gertha herself hid behind a boulder and then, when the robbers were looking the other way she escaped into the woods and ran and ran, and when at last she could run no further, she threw herself down on the grass and wept as if her heart would break. She had loved her master and mistress for they were all she had in the world.

But Gertha was as brave as she was gentle and kind and when darkness fell, she dried her eyes and said aloud, "I will stay where I am for there would be little chance of finding the way out of these woods now. Perhaps the good angels will take care of me."

No sooner had she spoken than a beautiful white dove flew down from one of the trees. It had a tiny golden key in its beak and this it put into Gertha's hand. Then it said softly into her ear, "Over there is a great tree and set in the tree is a little lock. Open it with this golden key and you will find something to eat."

Gertha took the key over to the tree, fitted it into the lock, and as she turned it a door swung open. Inside, she found a loaf of white bread and a bowl of creamy milk and she was so hungry and thirsty that she ate all the bread and drank all the milk there and then. But when she looked around for the dove to say thank you, she could not see it anywhere.

Later that night, the dove came to her again. It placed another tiny key in her hand and told her to go once more to the tree. "Open it," the dove said, quietly. "Inside you will find a bed where you can sleep."

Obediently, Gertha went to the tree and using her key, she opened it. Inside was a bed made up with fine linen sheets and it looked so comfortable and inviting that Gertha tumbled into it and fell fast asleep.

In the morning the dove came to her for the third time and for the third time it put a tiny key into her hand, saying, "Do you see that tree to the right of you? Open the door and you will find dresses to wear while you are in these woods."

Gertha obeyed and there, inside the tree, were so many wonderful dresses that she caught her breath in astonishment. "Any one of these will make me look like a Princess," she said out loud. Then she chose a dress of shimmering silver and blue and pulled it over her own shabby dress with its patched skirt. And, oh, how pretty she looked though there was no one to see.

As the days passed, Gertha no longer thought of trying to find her way out of the woods. The dove came to her each morning to see to her needs and although it never stayed longer than two hours, Gertha longed for its visits and in time grew to love the gentle bird.

One morning the dove said to her, "Will you do something for me?"

And Gertha answered, "I will do anything you ask – anything at all, so please what is it you want me to do?"

"I want you to follow me through the woods," said the dove.

"I will take you to a small house where an old woman lives."

"What shall I say to her?" Gertha wanted to know.

"Say nothing," the dove answered. "Do not speak a single word but pass her by on the right side and when you are in the house search for a room that is full of rings."

"What shall I do then?" Gertha asked.

"You must look for the plainest of the rings," said the dove. "You will see many rings that are so beautiful and so enriched with jewels that you will want to try them on. But if you care anything for me you will leave these beautiful rings and take the one that is without a stone and is plain and ordinary. Slip it on your little finger and come back to me here."

"I promise I will do as you say," Gertha whispered, already half afraid of the old woman she had not yet met. Could she be some kind of wicked witch? Before she had time to question the dove further, the bird flew away and Gertha was forced to run after it.

After what seemed a long time and when Gertha was beginning to feel she could scarcely take another step, the dove flew back to her. "Beyond that clump of trees stands the house. I can go no further. Remember what I have said. Take the plainest of the rings and speak no word."

The little house that Gertha came upon looked like any other, but the old woman who stood on the steps was ugly and bent and her red eyes were sharply inquisitive as they fixed themselves upon the girl. "Good-day to you," she croaked. "And what would you be wanting with me? Speak child! Don't be afraid."

But Gertha, remembering the dove's warning, answered not a single word. As quickly as she could, she passed the old woman on her right side and entered the house. Once inside, she ran from room to room until, at last, she came upon a room that was filled with rings.

Never in all her life had Gertha seen such wonderful rings. There were diamond rings, set in bands of twisted gold, that shimmered in the sunlight. Ruby rings that glowed as if they contained a secret fire, and rings set with pearls the size of pebbles. Some were so small they would only fit a child's finger but others were just right for her own slender hands. And, oh, how Gertha longed to try them on!

Just in time, she remembered the dove's warning and, with a sigh, she began to search for the plain, ordinary ring that the dove had told her about. But search as she might, there was no sign of a plain gold band among all the glittering rings that shimmered and sparkled on the table and on the chairs.

As she began, for the third time, to search the room, the old woman came to the open door. "Help yourself, child," she croaked. "I am too old for such pretty things. Tell me, which of the rings do you like the best?"

When Gertha made no reply, the old woman hobbled away and Gertha crept to the door to see what she would do next. She saw her stretch up and take a bird's wicker cage from a hook in the wall. And then she saw – and how her heart began to beat – that inside the cage was a small brown bird that held a plain gold ring in its beak!

Gertha sprang towards the old woman, snatched the cage from her hand and opened it. The witch tried to push her away, but Gertha was too strong and quick for her. In a trice, the ring was on her finger and she was running, running, running out of the house and away through the woods.

To her surprise and disappointment, the dove was not waiting for her when she got back. "I have the ring," she thought, "and I have done everything it asked. Why doesn't the dove come to me?" And because she was tired and disappointed she leaned against one of the trees and began silently to weep. Then something very wonderful happened. That self-same tree changed into a tall handsome young man, who put his arms around Gertha and began speaking to her — in the very voice the dove had used.

"Gertha! My little Gertha," he said. "I am your dove. You have freed me from an enchantment that held me bound for part of the day as a tree and for part of the day as a dove. The old woman was a witch who, out of spite against my father, the King, worked her evil spell on me. It could only be broken by a girl such as you who could find the ring and wear it on her little finger."

Then the King's son took Gertha out of the woods into his father's kingdom where, not long afterwards, they were happily married.

The Sleeping Beauty

THERE WAS once a King and a Queen who longed to have a child of their own more than anything else in the world. Imagine their joy when, one day, the Queen was told that at last she was going to have a baby.

"I should like a little girl," said the Queen.

The King said, "I should like a little boy but what does it matter? Boy or girl, we shall love our baby with all our hearts."

Well, the Queen's wish for a baby girl was granted and she was so lovely, even as a tiny baby, that the King completely forgot he had wanted a boy.

"We must hold a grand Christening Party," said the Queen. "All our friends will be invited, especially the Seven Good Fairies. They will be our guests of honor."

"I have already arranged that the Fairies shall each receive a golden spoon, fork and knife studded with diamonds and rubies," said the King.

The Queen clapped her hands in delight, "And to make it an even more attractive gift we will place them in a gold casket," she exclaimed. "The Fairies will be thrilled!"

On the day of the Christening Party, the palace was crowded with

people all dressed in their finest clothes. The Queen herself was radiant as she invited her guests to take their places at the long banqueting table. The Seven Good Fairies were among the last of the guests to arrive and they were immediately shown to their seats for the Queen was anxious to see their faces when they discovered the splendid gold caskets.

Just as the banquet was about to begin an ancient fairy, with an ugly wrinkled face and a long hooked nose, hobbled into the room. At the sight of the bent figure in the long dark cloak and tall black hat, the guests fell silent. Trembling with rage, the old fairy pointed to the gold caskets set out before the Good Fairies.

"I see no place laid for me," she croaked. "And where is my gold casket? Those who forget me pay dearly. . . ."

The Queen grew pale at the fairy's threatening words. "It is true," she said quickly, "that we did not think to invite you to our baby's Christening Party. We did not remember that you were still in our kingdom. But you are most welcome to sit down at table with us. . . ."

The ancient fairy shook her head. "I will not sit with you," she said angrily. "No place is laid; there is no gift for me. But I will stay. Yes, I will stay and bestow upon your precious child a gift – a very special gift – of my own." And she cackled.

So chilling were her words and so evil was her smile that the other guests could scarcely bring themselves to eat the wonderful dishes that were placed before them. And when the banquet at last came to an end, they hurried into the room where the baby Princess lay in her cradle.

"I must be the very last to bestow a gift upon the royal child," the youngest of the Good Fairies told herself, as she lingered behind the others. "I do not trust that wicked old crone."

Now it was the custom in those far-off days for the Good Fairies to give very special gifts to royal children. They were the kind of gifts that only the Fairies could give.

"You shall have great beauty," said one of the Good Fairies stepping forward and bending over the little Princess.

"You shall sing like the nightingale," said another.

"You shall dance like the wind," said the third.

"You will be gentle and kind," said the fourth.

"And perform every act with grace," said the fifth.

"You will be able to make music on any instrument," said the sixth fairy.

Scarcely had she finished speaking than the old fairy thrust her aside. Bending over the cradle, she bestowed her gift upon the little child: "You will die, die, die!" A gasp of horror went up from the guests, but the old fairy continued, "You will die the day you prick your finger with a spindle from a spinning wheel. . ."

In the silence that followed this terrible curse, the seventh and youngest of the Good Fairies cried, "Take comfort, your Majesties, the Princess shall not die. I have not yet bestowed my gift upon your daughter." And stepping to the cradle side, she said gently, "It is true that I have no power to undo the evil curse. But if your daughter pricks her finger with a spindle, I say she will not die. Instead, she will fall into a deep sleep that will endure for one hundred years. At the end of that time a king's son will wake her with a kiss."

The King and Queen were comforted by the Good Fairy's words and, the very next day, the King sent out a decree which said that all spinning wheels in the kingdom must be burned without delay. Any person found with a spinning wheel would be instantly put to death.

The Princess grew into the most beautiful, sweet-natured girl that had ever lived. She was loved by everyone and, as the years passed, the King and Queen almost forgot the wicked fairy's threat. No one had seen a spinning wheel for sixteen years or more and the Princess herself had never seen one.

One summer, when the countryside seemed more beautiful than usual, the King and Queen decided to take the Princess to one of their castles in the mountains. As soon as they arrived at the huge, old castle, the Princess immediately began to explore. Up, up, the long winding staircase she ran until, at last, she reached the turret rooms at the very top of the castle.

Pushing open one of the doors, she was surprised to see an old, white-haired woman sitting at a large wheel.

"What are you doing, old lady?" asked the Princess, looking curiously at the wheel. "What is that big wheel for?"

"It's a spinning wheel, child," said the old dame, who had no way of knowing she was addressing a Princess. "And I am spinning. For fifty years or more I have been in this tower busy at my spinning."

"Spinning?" repeated the Princess. "That's a word I have never heard before. But do let me try. It looks such fun!"

"You may try if you wish," said the old woman, smiling at the girl's eager face.

The Princess was in such a hurry that as she took hold of the spindle, it pricked her finger. Immediately she fell to the ground – her eyes closed.

Alarmed and shaken, the old woman stumbled to the top of the stairs, calling loudly for help. Servants came running, crowding and jostling each other in their efforts to be the first to reach the Princess and see what had happened. Some threw water on her face, while others ran to fetch the King and Queen.

When the royal couple saw their daughter lying on the ground, so still and with her eyes tightly shut, they remembered the wicked fairy's evil curse. "There is nothing we can do," the Queen choked through her tears. "Our daughter will now sleep for a hundred years."

Servants carried the Princess to the royal guest chambers and gently laid her upon a bed of gold and silver.

"She is almost more beautiful now than when she was alive," the Queen whispered, between sobs.

"But she is alive now, too," the King reminded her, gently. "Let us send for the youngest of the Good Fairies and ask her what we should do next."

The King sent his own personal Dwarf messenger to the Good Fairy, knowing that the Dwarf could cover the ground more swiftly than any ordinary mortal. And, within an hour, he had reached the Good Fairy. "I will come at once," she said, when she heard the King's message.

The Good Fairy made the journey to the castle in a chariot of fire drawn by two dragons.

"There is little I can do," the Good Fairy told the King, when she arrived at the castle. "But at least I can make it more pleasant for the Princess on her waking."

Taking her wand, the fairy floated around the castle. First she went down into the vast kitchens and there she gently tapped the cook, the scullery maids, the stewards and the sewing maids with her wand. Can you guess what happened? Each and every one of them fell fast asleep right in the middle of what they were doing. The cook dropped off to sleep with the soup ladle at his lips; the scullery maid fell asleep as she was drying one of the gold plates and the two sewing maids on their stools slept in the very act of threading their needles.

Pages, porters and ladies-in-waiting all slept where they stood or sat. Outside, in the courtyard, grooms fell fast asleep as they brushed

their horses' tails. Even the horses slept. Dogs, cats, hens, and the little birds in the trees were all soon silently sleeping.

When the fairy was satisfied that the whole castle was sound asleep, she returned to the King and Queen. "There is little left to do," she said. "When your daughter wakes up, the castle will come to life again as well and she will not feel strange or lonely."

After thanking the good fairy, they left the castle and rode away in their coach and the fairy climbed into her chariot of fire, drawn by the two dragons. Her task was almost done. Only one thing more must she do before she left. Using her magic powers, the fairy then raised a tangled mass of brambles and prickly bushes all around the castle so that all within might sleep undiscovered and undisturbed.

A hundred years passed. The King and Queen and all the Princess's uncles and aunts were long since dead. Another King ruled over the land and he knew nothing of the sleeping Princess in the woods.

Now this King had a tall handsome son who was very fond of hunting and, one day, while in the woods, the Prince found his way barred by a forest of bushes and brambles.

"What do you think lies beyond this tangled growth?" The Prince asked one of his huntsmen. "For a moment I thought I saw the glint of a castle tower through the branches."

The huntsman shook his head but an old woodcutter heard the Prince's question and spoke up. "Some say an ogre lived in the castle once," he told the Prince. "Others declare it is haunted by ghosts and witches. Who knows?"

"I believe neither in ghosts nor witches," laughed the Prince. "Come, old man, rack your brains. There must be some other more likely tale connected with this place."

The old woodcutter hesitated. "Many long years ago," he began slowly, "my father did tell me a strange story of a beautiful Princess who was left inside the castle, fast asleep. He talked of some wicked enchantment that held her in its power."

The young Prince laughed again. "Here then is an adventure more exciting than a day's hunting," he cried merrily. "A beautiful Princess, you say? Then I will break through this great tangle of bushes and find out for myself."

With that, the Prince drew his sword and prepared to strike a trail through the thorny bushes. To his astonishment they parted before he touched them and there before him lay a winding path through their midst.

More astonished than ever, but still unafraid, the Prince followed the path until at last he came to the castle itself. What a strange and

49

awesome sight met his eyes. There, about the courtyard, lay dogs and cats sleeping soundly; but it was not just the sight of the sleeping animals that made him wonder if it was he who was dreaming. Grooms, their arms raised as if in the very act of attending their horses, stood there motionless, their eyes shut. An eerie stillness hung about the courtyard and about the castle itself as the Prince pushed open the creaking door.

Everywhere he went it was the same story. "It is true, then," he thought. "This castle is under some evil spell. But where is the beautiful Princess?"

In the last room he went into he found her, lying on a bed of silver and gold, and the Prince, as he walked towards her, caught his breath. She was a thousand times more lovely than any girl he had ever seen.

Tenderly he bent over her and kissed the pale face of the sleeping girl. No sooner had his lips brushed her cheek, than the Princess sighed deeply. Then she opened her eyes and sat up.

"So you have come at long last," she whispered softly, holding out her arms to him. "I have waited a hundred years for you."

And as she spoke the whole castle came to life. The cook finished tasting his soup – which was very cold – the sewing maids threaded their needles, and stewards and porters rushed hither and thither. In the courtyard dogs barked, cats miaowed and the grooms attended to the horses.

Presently, a lady-in-waiting entered the room to ask if the Princess would like her hair brushed as usual, and the Princess smiled and nodded just as if she had never been asleep.

By the end of that strange day the Prince had declared his love for the Princess and the next morning they were married in the castle's chapel. Never had the Princess looked more beautiful although her wedding gown was a hundred years old!

And at the end of a week of blissful happiness, the Prince told his new wife that soon he must return home.

"I cannot take you with me," he said. "My mother is a strange and jealous woman and would not welcome you. It is best that you remain here in the castle until I judge the time is right."

The Princess willingly agreed for the Prince went on to promise that he would come and see her every day.

When the Prince returned to his home, his mother looked at him with angry, questioning eyes. But he dared not tell her of his secret marriage for he was frightened of what she might do to his lovely wife.

Two years passed. Each day the Prince visited the castle and each day he grew more in love. Now he was the proud father of two children, a pretty little girl called Dawn and a handsome boy called Day.

When his children were about three or four years old, the Prince's father died, and the Prince was proclaimed the new King. Now, he decided, the moment had come when he could safely take his wife and family back to the palace.

From the moment the beautiful young Queen entered the palace, the Queen-Mother hated her. So deep and terrible was this hatred that in time she became more and more of an ogress, possessing cruel and frightening powers.

One day the King was forced to leave his family for his country was at war and the soldiers had asked that he lead them into battle. "I

leave my beloved wife and my two dear children in your care," he said to his mother, little knowing how she felt about them. "Take good care of them for I love them with all my heart."

No sooner had the young King ridden away than the black-hearted old Queen-Mother sent for her daughter-in-law and the two children.

"We shall spend the next few weeks in my house in the country," the Queen-Mother said. "We shall be safer there."

Almost as soon as the family was settled in a lonely house in the forest, the Queen-Mother sent for one of her servants. "For my supper tonight," she told the huntsman, "I will eat little Dawn."

The huntsman could only stare at the Queen-Mother in speechless horror. For the first time, he saw how long and yellow her teeth were and how she now seemed to be more an ogress than a human-being.

"I cannot do such a dreadful thing," he began to protest. But his mistress cut him short.

"It is your life or the child's," she threatened, and the servant fled from the room.

On his return to his cottage at the bottom of the garden, the poor man confided in his wife. "I love the child," he said. "Since she came here only a few days ago she has quite won me over with her gentle winning ways."

"Then we must think of a way to save her," said his wife, who was a kind-hearted country woman.

At last the huntsman decided what to do. He killed a young lamb and brought it to his wife. The good woman cooked it and then made a tasty sauce, heavily spiced, which she poured over the meat.

"Take that to your mistress," she told her husband. "But before you do, bring the child to me and I will hide her in our cottage."

The Queen-Mother ate the dish with relish that night and the huntsman prayed that it might be the end of the affair. But the next day, she sent for him again.

"I will have Day for my supper tonight," she told him, and she looked more than ever like an ogress.

"We must trick her again," said the huntsman's wife. "Bring the boy here and I will hide him."

This time the servant killed a young goat and his wife cooked the meat for many hours in her oven.

Once again, the wicked Queen-Mother was deceived, vowing that she had enjoyed her supper exceedingly well. But, oh dear, worse was to come. She had, so she thought, destroyed the Queen's children. Now she would put an end to the Queen herself, the woman her son loved so much.

"I will have the Queen herself tonight for my supper," she told the huntsman when, once again, he stood before her. "Then, indeed, I shall be at peace."

This time the servant knew that it would be very hard to deceive the ogress, for the Queen, though very beautiful, was more than a hundred years old.

"Our terrible mistress will expect the meat to be tough," he re-

minded his wife, as they talked together later that day. "It is not likely we can work the same trick three times over. This time I must carry out her orders. It is my life or the Queen's." And with that, he grabbed his long hunting knife and rushed from the cottage.

He found the young Queen seated by the window. She was weeping bitterly for she believed that she had lost her two children forever.

"I know what you have come to do," she said softly. "Take my life. I give it to you gladly for my children are dead and I have nothing to live for." Then she fell on her knees, baring her slender neck.

The kind-hearted huntsman was so overcome by the beautiful Queen's grief that he cried, "Do not weep so, your Majesty. Your children are alive and well, hidden in my cottage. Let me take you there and I will find some way to trick my evil mistress."

On hearing this joyful news, the Queen sprang to her feet and willingly followed the servant to his cottage where she was reunited with her two children. Then the huntsman went into the forest, caught and killed a young deer and his wife roasted it with such skill that when the meat was ready it was part-tough and part-tender.

So, once again, the wicked Queen-Mother was deceived and after her supper, she sent for the huntsman and complimented him on the way he had carried out her orders. "When my son returns from the wars," she said finally, "you will tell him that a pack of hungry wolves attacked the Queen and the children as they walked in the forest and devoured them."

Who knows what might have happened if the ogress had not, one day, chosen to walk in the garden close to the cottage. Suddenly she heard and recognized Dawn's childish laughter and knew, in a flash, that she had been tricked.

Trembling with rage, her face all shades of black and purple, she had the little family brought to her. Then she had a deep pit dug and she filled it with all sorts of hideous creatures such as snakes, vipers and giant toads. "Now I will see you perish with my own eyes!" cried the ogress.

Scarcely were the words out of her mouth than the King himself strode into the garden. Having returned victorious from the wars, he had come with all speed to find his wife and children. Never again could the ogress hope to deceive her son for now he was seeing for himself her true nature. With a piercing shriek, she turned away from him and cast herself into the deep pit where she was instantly devoured by the waiting vipers.

So, after all, the story of the Sleeping Beauty of the Woods ended happily. The King took her back to his palace, vowing that never again would he leave her and, as far as we know, he kept his promise.

The Elf-Hill

I F Y O U search long and carefully you may come upon the old elf-hill of this story. It stands close to a wood and not very far from the sea. It is not very tall but it is round and smooth, with a secret door through which the elf maid passes when she has business with the outside world.

Two lizards happened to be near the elf-hill when, one afternoon, it opened and an elf maid came tripping out. She was the old Elf King's housekeeper and she was clearly in a hurry as she ran past the lizards on her way to the sea.

"Something is going on inside the old elf-hill," said one lizard to the other. "I wonder what it can be."

"If we wait around we may find out," said the other. "The elf maid has gone down to the sea to speak to the Night Raven. I'm certain of it."

While the lizards talked together, the elf maid had reached the sea and there was the Night Raven sitting on a stone.

"You are invited to the elf-hill this evening," said the elf maid, "but I want you to do something for me. We shall have a number of important guests and I would be greatly obliged if you would attend to the invitations."

"Who is coming?" asked the Night Raven.

"I have had some argument with the Elf King over the list of guests," said the elf maid. "But it's settled now. The Merman and his daughters are invited. And as they will not be happy on dry land I am arranging that they have wet stones to sit on. We are also inviting the King of the High Mountains, a jolly old gnome who they say is looking for a wife. Our King has seven daughters – all unmarried – so we shall see. And then there will be a number of magicians . . ."

"Croak!" said the Raven, and away he flew to give out the invitations.

That night the great hall of the elf-hill was decorated for the occasion; the floor had been washed with moonshine and the walls rubbed with some special witches' polish so that they glowed like tulips in the light. Mushroom spawn and frogs' legs were tossed into great plates of green salad and there were bottles of deep red blackberry juice and beer for the King of the High Mountains. The Elf King wore a slate crown – very tall and shiny – and there was a pleasant scent of burning horse-hair everywhere.

The Elf King's daughters, as they waited for their guests to arrive, looked extremely pretty in their shawls of gossamer which were borrowed from the spiders.

"When will he come, this King of the Mountains?" asked the youngest, who longed to be married and so escape from the elf-hill.

"That depends on the wind and the weather," said the Elf King. "But you'll like him, I'm sure, for he is merry and honest. What's more he has many rock castles and a gold mine. And, he has two sons who most likely will accompany him."

As he spoke, two Will-o'-the-Wisps came hopping up in great excitement. "They're coming! They're coming," they cried.

"Let me stand in the moonshine and welcome them," said the old Elf King, straightening his crown.

The grand old gnome of the mountains wore a crown of polished fir cones and a bear-skin and tall warm boots and very noble did he look as he greeted the Elf King. Then the two Kings went into the elf-hill together and behind them followed the gnome's sons, rough-looking fellows with bare heads and strong arms and legs.

All the other guests were already waiting, and all were thoughtfully arranged. The Merman and his family sat at the table in huge washing tubs looking very happy, while the magicians had already begun their entertainment. The Night Raven kept out of the way by perching on a stool.

The Elf King sat at the top of the long table and beside him sat his most honored guest, the King of the Mountains, who took off his thick fur coat. His two sons took off their boots and put their feet on the table, which was not the way true gentlemen should behave, but nothing was said.

Then the Elf King's daughters appeared and danced in a charming way which delighted the old gnome, who had never seen girls dance before. "What else can they do?" he asked, for of course he was thinking that he did not want a wife who was only good at dancing.

"You shall see," said their father proudly. "But first let us hear from you."

So then the old gnome told them stories of his mountains; how it was in the winter when the bells on the sledges sounded. And how at certain times, the great salmon leaped up against the falling water, and how waterfalls rushed down over the rocks with white foam and a noise like thunder.

"Bravo!" said the Elf King, when the mountain gnome came to the end of his stories. And he told his housekeeper to bring in the wine and the plates of salad with the frogs' legs and mushroom spawn.

After the feasting, the Elf King presented his daughters, one by one. The youngest was as light and graceful as a moonbeam and she curtseyed low in front of the old gnome, whirled around twice and was gone, completely vanished, which was something she could do very well. But the old King of the Mountains said that he did not think he would care for a vanishing wife. "I don't think my sons would like it either," he said. "After all, she is to be a mother to them and mothers should always be there, not up to any disappearing tricks."

The second daughter fared no better in the gnome's eyes for she was an acrobat and her bending and leaping and twisting in the air quite alarmed him.

"Wait until you meet my third daughter," said the Elf King. "She has learned the art of cooking from the Moor Woman and knows how to stuff oak leaves and bake delicious mixtures."

"She would certainly make a good housekeeper," said the Elf

King, after he had met her. "But from what she said, she goes in for fancy cooking and my sons like plain solid food."

Now it was the turn of the fourth daughter. She came carrying a great harp and as soon as she struck the first chord, everybody in the hall sprang to their feet and began to hop about. Even the old gnome and the Elf King were forced to jig and hop.

"Enough!" cried the Elf King at last. Then turning to the gnome, who was quite out of breath, he said, "This is her gift. Whenever she plays on her harp, those who hear must dance and jig."

"She wouldn't do at all for me," said the Mountain King. "Quite unsuitable. I have no wish to find myself hopping and jigging whenever she chooses. No, no, I consider her a dangerous woman – What can your next daughter do?"

"I love the mountains," answered the girl, speaking for herself. "I will be safe and happy only if I can go to the mountains with you."

"She only wants to go with you because she is afraid the elf-hill might disappear into the earth one day," whispered her youngest sister. "She thinks the mountains will last forever . . ."

"If that's the only reason," said the old gnome, "I want none of her."

The sixth daughter would have none of the Old Gnome. "I don't want to marry," she said. "So don't ask me."

Now it was the turn of the seventh daughter. "What can you do?" asked the King of the Mountains.

"I can tell you as many stories as you have fingers on your hands," said she, with a merry smile. And she took the gnome's hands in hers which pleased him greatly. Then she began to tell him wonderful stories – stories of witches and ghosts and Will-o'-the-Wisps and moonshine, one story for each finger.

When, at last, she came to the finger on which sat a broad gold ring, the gnome cried, "Stop! Take the ring. I will have you as my wife. I will hear no more stories now, but when we are home you will tell your stories, for no one in the mountains can spin a tale like you. We shall be happy together."

Then the old gnome and the Elf King's seventh and eldest daughter danced around together and the Merman and his family applauded loudly, clapping their tails against the wash tubs.

"What about your sons?" asked the Elf King hopefully, when the dance was over. "Will they consider two of my other daughters?"

"One wedding in the family is enough," said the gnome, "and

besides you can see for yourself how it is with them. They are not interested."

This was true, for the two big boys were fast asleep with their heads on the table. They awoke with the sound of the cock crowing, and the Elf King's housekeeper came in and said, "Now we must close up the shutters, so that the sun will not burn us. The feasting is over. It's time for everybody to go home."

So then the elf-hill opened for the last time and the black Raven, who had sat for the most part in a corner, went with the Merman and his family down to the sea. And the old gnome and his two sons wrapped themselves up in their furs and left in a hurry, the Elf King's seventh daughter running behind them.

All this was seen by the two lizards who enjoyed every moment of it. "I told you," said one, "that something very strange was going on inside the elf-hill, didn't I?"

"You did," said the other. "And you were right. It looks as if the Elf King has lost a daughter. But then he's got that old gnome for a son. That's what they say, 'lose a daughter and gain a son.'"

Then the two lizards, as soon as the elf-hill closed up, ran off to look for their breakfast.

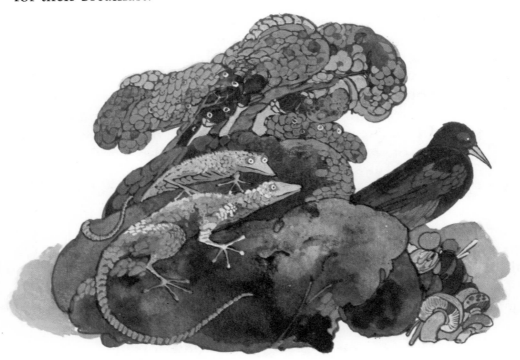

The Robber's Treasure

ONCE UPON a time there were two brothers. One was so rich that he rode everywhere in a carriage, entertained at his home twice a week and drank nothing but wine with his meals. But in spite of his wealth he gave nothing away. The other brother, in contrast, was so poor that his most valued possession was an old barrow. In good times, he could afford to feed his wife and children, but more often than not, he went hungry himself.

The two brothers rarely met, for the rich merchant would not trouble with a poor relation who was no better than a peddlar. Whenever he saw his young brother in the street, he would look the other way.

One day the poor brother took his barrow into the forest hoping to fill it with sticks that he could sell in the market. Things had gone badly for him over the past month and he was worried that he might not be able to provide for his family. He was so deep in thought, that he scarcely noticed where he was going until he found himself facing a tall bare-looking mountain that he could not remember seeing before.

As the poor brother stood there staring at the strange mountain, he saw, in the distance, a company of men coming towards him. "These men could easily be a band of robbers," he thought. So quickly he hid his barrow in the bushes and climbed into a tree so that they would pass without seeing him. When they drew close, he saw that they wore great gold hoops in their ears and colored sashes around their waists in which were stuck long knives. There was no doubt at all that they were robbers and the poor man was thankful that he was hidden.

To his surprise, the robbers stopped when they reached the mountain. Then their leader, a tall fierce-looking man with a black beard and glittering eyes, shouted, "Semsi mountain, Semsi mountain, open yourself!" And at once the mountain opened down the middle. The poor brother could scarcely believe his eyes at this but he counted the

robbers as they disappeared inside. There were twelve of them and when the last had disappeared the mountain closed up again.

Trembling with a mixture of excitement and fear, the poor brother stayed where he was in the tree until, after a short time, the mountain opened again and the robbers appeared, each carrying a heavy sack on his shoulders. When all twelve were outside, their leader shouted, "Semsi mountain, Semsi mountain, shut yourself!" And the gap in the mountain closed. Then laughing and joking, the robbers made off through the forest.

As soon as the noise of their laughter had died away, the peddlar climbed down and ran over to the mountain. "Semsi mountain, Semsi mountain, open yourself!" he cried, trembling with excitement. And the mountain opened.

Oh, what a sight met his eyes as he went inside! He was standing in a cave that was filled with treasure. Gold and silver spilled out of huge brass-bound chests; precious stones, diamonds, rubies and pearls lay in neat piles about the floor and there were, besides, all manner of rich ornaments – bracelets and necklaces such as an Empress might wear.

The poor man gasped, his eyes dazzled by so much splendor. Then, recovering his wits, he went over to one of the chests and began to fill his pockets with gold pieces. When his pockets were bulging, he looked longingly at the precious stones but decided wisely to leave them in their neat piles.

The mountain had closed up behind him but the poor brother, for all his excitement, had not forgotten the password. "Semsi mountain, Semsi mountain, open yourself!" he said, and the mountain opened. Once outside, he said, "Semsi mountain, Semsi mountain, shut yourself," and the mountain closed up once more.

Never had the way home seemed so long as the poor man trundled his barrow through the forest. All his worries were over. The gold would buy food and clothing for his family and there would be plenty to spare for those of his friends who were poorer than himself.

The next few months passed most pleasantly for the poor brother and

his family. He moved to a bigger house, bought better clothes for himself and his family and was generous to all his friends. He told no one about the mountain except his wife, and it was she who said to him one day, "Husband, we have only a few pieces of gold left. What shall we do when it is all gone?"

"I will return to the mountain," said the poor man. "There is no danger if I keep a sharp look-out for the robbers. They may not even have missed the gold."

"This time take a bushel measure with you," advised his wife. "That will hold all the gold you need and give you an idea of how much you are taking."

Now the poor man did not own a measure and so he went to his brother to borrow one. The merchant was curious to know how his brother had become so well-to-do and eyed his new suit jealously. But the poor man would not answer his questions and finally the merchant gave him the measure.

Once inside the mountain, the poor man took only the gold though it seemed to him that the cave was ablaze with light from the precious stones. When his measure was full, he stepped outside, closed the mountain with the magic password and hurried home. Once again, all went well. Encouraged by his wife, the poor brother bought a carriage and pair and took his family to church every Sunday. Still he did not forget the poor of the town and he made himself responsible for a number of families.

With so many calls on his money, it was not surprising that before long it began to run out. "Borrow the measure again," said his wife. "It is best if you take only a little at a time."

The rich merchant was now green with envy and when his brother called he asked him all kinds of questions in an effort to find out where the money was coming from. But each time, the poor brother answered with a joke, which greatly irritated his brother.

"Then tell me," the merchant shouted at last, "why do you want my bushel measure? Has it got something to do with your good fortune?"

"I – er – want to measure some barley," said the poor brother, caught unawares by the question.

"I'll fetch it then," said the merchant, pretending to believe him. But before giving the measure to his brother he covered the bottom with tar.

"Now we shall see what sticks to the tar," he whispered to his wife. "I'm certain it won't be barley!"

The peddlar thanked his brother and set out immediately for the mountain. For the third time he was successful in taking the gold without seeing the robbers and thankfully he returned home. Then he emptied out the gold and took the measure back to his brother. But alas, all unbeknown to him, a single gold piece had stuck to the tar and the merchant was quick to discover it.

"Now you'll have to tell me the truth," he said, as he faced his young brother. "If you don't tell me where this gold came from, I'll take it to the justice of peace. For all I know, you may be a robber in disguise."

The poor brother saw that he was beaten and he began telling his story. "Of course, there is no way of getting in or out of that mountain," he finished, "except by using the magic words. Semsi is a queer name for a mountain to be sure, but there you are."

"You were a fool not to help yourself to the diamonds and the rubies!" exclaimed the merchant. "I'll not make the same mistake." And he rushed out of the house.

The merchant had no difficulty in finding the mountain and he was so greedy for the treasure that he forgot all about the robbers themselves. "Semsi mountain, Semsi mountain, open yourself!" he shouted. And the mountain opened down the middle.

"That brother of mine did not lie," cried the merchant when he saw the diamonds, the rubies and the pearls.

So greedy and eager was he to fill the sack he had with him, that he stumbled and almost fell as he reached out to take a handful of precious stones. Working like a madman, he filled his sack to overflowing and then stuffed his pockets until they bulged at the seams. He lost all count of time and forgot everything except the fortune that lay all around him. When at last he was satisfied that he could not push another pearl into his sack he staggered to the front of the cavern and shouted, "Simeli mountain, Simeli mountain, open yourself!" Nothing happened. He had forgotten the mountain's right name!

In sudden despair, the rich man shouted, "Simeli! Smelimi! Semili!" and a dozen other names but never the right one. His face grew white with fear; he was trapped. His new-found wealth was of no use to him now. Hours passed and the merchant was hoarse with shouting. At last, at the end of the day, the mountain opened and the robbers came in. The merchant cried out in terror at the sight of them and dropped to his knees.

"So we have caught our thief at last!" cried the robber leader. "Now we can take our revenge."

"Mercy!" whispered the rich man, "I did not steal your gold. It was my brother. Set me free and I'll show you where to find him."

But the robbers did not believe him, and really you couldn't blame them, for there was the merchant's sack full of precious stones and his pockets stuffed with gold. And so, being men of action, the robbers cut off his head.

When the merchant did not return, his brother guessed that he had been caught by the robbers. In deep sorrow he sent for his brother's widow and offered her a place in his own home and from then on took care of her as one of the family. Never again did he visit the mountain, but like a wise man, took better care of his gold and with the money from his brother's business, he managed very well for the rest of his days.

Little Tom Thumb

ONCE UPON a time there was a little boy who, when he was born, was no bigger than his father's thumb. So his father called him Tom Thumb and hoped that one day he would grow to be as big as his brothers. But, of course, he never did.

This story is all about little Tom Thumb and how he got the better of a cruel boy-eating ogre. It happened like this. Tom Thumb's father was a woodcutter. He was a good man but very poor and one winter, when the snow was on the ground, he found he had not enough money to buy a loaf of bread for his growing family.

"It's no use, wife," he said one day. "Here we are with seven little mouths to feed and I can't make enough to buy a loaf of bread."

"We must manage somehow," said his wife. "There's one thing, Tom Thumb doesn't eat more than a sparrow."

"That's true," admitted her husband. "But his six brothers have big appetites and I cannot bear to sit here and watch them starve. No, wife, my mind is made up."

Well, husband and wife talked and talked until finally the wood-cutter said what was in his mind. "As soon as the snow clears," he said, "I mean to take the boys deep into the forest and leave them there."

Now Tom Thumb had fallen asleep under his father's stool that night but when his mother began to weep and his father began to shout, he woke up. As he listened to them he soon realized what his father meant to do so he kept very still and quiet until both his parents left the room.

It was lucky for Tom's six brothers that he was so clever and that he could work out a plan to save them from being lost. As soon as the first sunny morning came along, Tom Thumb filled his pockets with small white stones. He guessed, you see, that this would be the morning his father would take them into the forest.

"Your father is going to take you into the forest today," their mother told the boys, and she gave them some hot milk. "You'll be able to play your games and have lots of fun." But she looked so sad and her eyes were so red that Peter, the eldest, asked, "If we're going to have fun why do you look so sad and why are your eyes red?" But their poor mother turned away, unable to answer.

Tom Thumb knew why, but he kept silent as his father told his sons to follow him into the forest. Well, they did have fun to begin with, playing hide-and-seek among the trees and running and jumping over the grass. But towards the end of the afternoon they were so tired that the woodcutter said, "We'll stop here for a rest. Build a fire and I will go further on to look for sticks."

The woodcutter walked away and Tom Thumb knew that he never meant to return. But he helped his brothers to start a fire, then he said, "Come on, boys! Let's sit around the fire and tell stories."

When it grew really dark and the owls began to hoot in the trees, Peter shivered, "I want to go home now," he said. "Why doesn't our father come back?"

"Perhaps the wolves have eaten him," said Johnny, who was the second youngest.

At the very idea of their father being eaten by wolves, all the boys except little Tom Thumb began to cry.

"What crybabies you are!" exclaimed Tom. "As soon as it is morning, we'll easily find our own way home and our father will be there to welcome us."

Comforted by their tiny brother's words, the others fell asleep and in the morning Tom showed them the little white stones he had dropped along the path as they had come through the forest. "We'll follow the stones," he told them. "They will show us the way back to our cottage."

Well, that is how clever Tom Thumb brought his brothers safely home. But soon after his father took the children into the forest again. Tom didn't have time to gather stones first. Instead he hastily snatched up some bread and this time he left a trail of breadcrumbs. Alas, the hungry forest birds ate the crumbs almost as soon as he let them fall.

This time the woodcutter took his children into a very dark part of the forest where the great trees grew so thickly together that they almost blotted out the sun. And soon he left them as he had done before. And this time they really were lost.

"We'll wait until morning," said Tom, as his brothers crowded around him. "Then we'll find our way back home just as we did last time."

But Tom Thumb had forgotten all about the hungry birds and when morning came he searched in vain for his trail of breadcrumbs. "Don't cry," he said to Peter, who was always the first to burst into tears. "We'll soon find a path that takes us home."

How dark and stormy it was as the children began to run through the trees! Then it started to rain and the rain blinded their eyes and made the forest grass so slippery that they were always falling down. At last, even brave little Tom began to lose heart. "I'll climb that tall tree over there," he said, trying to sound cheerful. "I'll be like a sailor climbing the mast of some big ship. The higher I climb the more I shall see."

His brothers watched as he clambered up the tall tree and they began to smile and throw their wooly caps in the air as suddenly they heard him shout: "Light ahoy! There's a house somewhere among the trees."

The boys crowded around him, as Tom clambered down. "Is it a light from our cottage window?" Peter wanted to know. But Tom shook his head.

"No," he said. "But that does not matter. We can ask for shelter and then tomorrow we will ask the way."

In good spirits, the brothers set off once again and now it didn't matter about the dark stormy sky or the heavy rain that beat down on their heads. But when, at last, they came upon the tall gray house that looked more like a castle, they were all very tired and soaked through to the skin.

With his brothers lined up behind him, Tom knocked on the great oak door. There was a long silence, then the door slowly opened and a tall thin woman stood looking down at them.

"Please," said Tom Thumb, "Can you give us something to eat and some shelter for the night?"

The woman shook her head. "You poor lambs," she said, "if I took you in now I would not be doing you a kindness. This is the house of a terrible ogre who is at present out hunting. No, no, get away from this place as fast as you can."

"I'm sorry, ma'am," said Tom, "but we're far too tired and hungry to go anywhere. If you don't take us in we shall all perish in this forest."

The woman hesitated. "I am the ogre's wife," she said at last. "I know my husband's ways. Why, if you were caught inside the house, it's more than likely he would eat you all one by one for his supper."

"We'll take that chance," said Tom. "Please let us come inside."

Now the ogre's wife was a kind-hearted woman even though she was married to a boy-eating ogre and Tom's little face, under his wooly cap, was so pleading that at last she opened the door a little more and said, "Very well. Come in, all of you. Perhaps there will be time for me to give you a bowl of hot porridge before the ogre comes home."

Tom followed the ogre's wife into a vast kitchen where a whole sheep was turning on a spit over a great fire. Then the woman sat them down at a long table and quickly put bowls of steaming porridge in front of them. How quickly they ate it up and how quickly, too, they began to smile and joke among themselves in the warm kitchen.

"I have always wanted pretty little boys of my own," the ogre's wife told them, as she filled up their bowls for a second time. "Alas, I have only seven great big ugly daughters who are already asleep upstairs. . ." She broke off, suddenly, at the sound of a thundering knock on the door. "It's – it's my husband," she whispered. "Quick – hide! Under that long couch over there!" As the boys ran to the couch, the woman cleared the table. Then straightening her apron, she went to the door and opened it.

As soon as the terrible ogre entered the kitchen he shouted for his supper. "It's quite ready, husband," said his wife. "You can see for yourself that the sheep is roasted and ready for eating."

The giant grunted as he sat down at table and his wife placed half the sheep in front of him. Presently, however, he raised his head and began sniffing. "Fee, fo, fum," he roared, "I smell – I smell. . ."

"You smell the roasting meat, that's all," said his wife quickly. "Now eat your supper while it is hot."

But the ogre was not satisfied. He searched the kitchen with his eyes until at last they became fixed on the couch. Then he rose to his feet, pushing the table away from him, and with two strides he was beside

the couch. One after another, he grabbed the boys and pulled them out.

"Oho!" he shouted. "So this is what you have hidden away, wife! Human boys – small and tender. How delicious they will be! Why, I have a good mind to eat you along with them, woman, except that your skin is yellow and wrinkled and would most likely taste unpleasant."

Tom Thumb on hearing these terrible words began begging for mercy. "Eat me, if you will," he said, "but spare my six brothers. They have done you no harm. And if you will only let them go you will never set eyes on them again."

The ogre laughed loudly at this. He held them up, one at a time in his great hands, then flung them into a corner. "Stay there," he said, "while I get my sharp hunting knife."

"Why not leave them until morning?" said his wife. "Your supper is growing cold; there is no need for such haste."

Now the thought of the tender tasty meal that he could look forward to in the morning had put the ogre into a very good temper.

"You are right," he said. "I'll leave them until the morning. I'll have them roasted for my breakfast; that will give you time to make a really good sauce for them."

Tom Thumb sighed with relief when he heard these words and seeing that the ogre was no longer paying much attention to them, he whispered to the ogre's wife to take them out of the kitchen.

"You can sleep in the same room as my daughters," she told the boys. "There's a big double bed in their room which my husband keeps for his grandmother."

The ogre's seven daughters were fast asleep in their own huge bed as Tom and his brothers entered the room. Tom saw, at a glance, how ugly they were with their hooked noses, cruel fang-like teeth and very big mouths. Indeed, they were so like their father that already they were beginning to eat little boys for breakfast too.

"My husband likes them to wear their gold crowns even when they are sleeping," the ogre's wife whispered, as she tucked the boys into the bed. "Do not talk among yourselves for I'm afraid my daughters, though still quite small, are nearly as fierce as their father."

Tom Thumb lay wide awake wondering how he could save his brothers, who had cried themselves softly to sleep. "Supposing the ogre changes his mind," he suddenly thought, "and comes upstairs with his sharp hunting knife to cut our throats. How shall we defend ourselves?"

Then he had a brilliant idea and, getting out of bed, he tiptoed over to the bed that held the ogre's sleeping daughters. Gently, oh so gently, he removed their crowns of gold and placed his brothers' wooly caps on their heads. Then, smiling to himself, he put their golden crowns on his brothers' heads. "Now if the ogre should come with his knife," he thought, "he will surely feel for the heads that wear the caps." Then, tired out, he fell fast asleep.

How long Tom Thumb slept he had no idea but he awoke to hear the clock downstairs strike midnight. Then he heard something else. Somebody terribly heavy was coming up the stairs. Under his weight the stairs creaked and groaned as if they were complaining. "So I was right," Tom thought. "The ogre has changed his mind about eating us for breakfast. He's going to eat us now."

Presently, the door opened and Tom knew the ogre was in the room, but it was so dark that the giant had to feel his way around. He was very sleepy and very slow as he came into the room for he had drunk a great deal of wine with his supper. When he came to the bed where Tom lay with his brothers, the ogre stretched out a huge hand and touched – what do you think – the golden crowns!

"Wrong bed!" he grunted. "M-must be the other!" And he stumbled clumsily across the room. Although he felt more than usually sleepy, he remembered quite clearly that the boys had been wearing bright wooly caps. When his groping fingers felt something soft and warm he muttered, "Right bed! Wooly caps! Now I've got the rascals!"

He raised his knife and, oh dear me, he cut off the heads of his seven sleeping daughters! This deed done, the ogre gave a mighty yawn and then decided that really he was far too sleepy to enjoy a meal at such a late hour. "I'll leave my wife to see to it in the morning," he told himself, as he left the room.

No sooner had he gone than Tom Thumb sprang from the bed. "Wake up! Wake up!" he whispered to his brothers. "We must escape now. Tomorrow will be too late."

His brothers woke at once, shivering and frightened. "Follow me," Tom told them. "The ogre's gone to bed. He thinks we're dead so he is no longer on his guard."

Then he led his brothers downstairs and out of the back door. As silent as mice, they crept through the garden and climbed over the wall.

"Now we must run," said Tom. "We must run and run as fast as we can until we are far away from this terrible place."

The brothers ran as fast as their trembling legs would carry them all through the night, stopping only for short rests. They didn't dare sit down for long.

Meanwhile, as soon as it was light the ogre awoke and began to

think, with pleasure, of the feast that he was soon to have. "Go upstairs
and get the boys ready," he told his wife. And his wife, not knowing
the sight that was to meet her eyes, obeyed. When she saw what had
happened to her seven daughters, she screamed loudly. Her screams
soon brought the ogre into the room, and one glance was enough to
show him how he had been tricked into killing his own daughters.

"Where did they get these wooly caps?" asked the wife stupidly.
But the ogre was in too much of a rage to answer. "I'll catch them, never
fear!" he shouted. "Fetch me my seven-league boots."

The ogre had won his seven-league boots in battle and they were
more precious to him than the bags of gold he kept under the floorboards. They were magic, you see, and could carry whoever wore

them seven leagues – which is a very long way – with a single stride.

In his wonderful boots, the ogre strode up and down the forest searching in vain for Tom Thumb and his brothers. Then he left the forest and strode up and down the countryside and he was such a terrifying sight that everybody ran indoors and hid under their beds.

Now it is a very well known fact that anyone who wears seven-league boots grows tired very easily and by the end of the morning the ogre was quite worn out. He was also very angry that he was taking so long to catch the boys. In fact he was so furious that he got very short of breath and so, to give himself a bit of a rest, he sat down close to a huge rock.

Tom Thumb and his brothers were short of breath too and they had chosen that very rock to shelter under while Tom Thumb kept a look-out.

"Don't move or speak," Tom whispered, when he saw the ogre.

His brothers were too scared to do anything except huddle together. But not Tom Thumb! As soon as he saw the ogre close his eyes and begin to doze, he crept out of his hiding-place and climbed the nearest tree. There, to his great joy, was his father's cottage. It was so close that he could see the smoke from the chimney curling up into the sky.

"We're nearly home," he whispered to his brothers, when he returned to them. "As soon as the ogre begins to snore, you must creep out of this hiding-place, up that short hill behind you and then down the other side. Promise me you'll do that. Our father's cottage is at the bottom of the hill. You'll be safe there."

Then little Tom Thumb, not a bit afraid, went up to the sleeping ogre and gently pulled off his boots. Now the boots being magic always fitted their wearer so when Tom put them on they shrank to a tiny size.

In his seven-league boots Tom Thumb covered the miles back to the ogre's house in a flash. When the ogre's wife saw him standing at the door, wearing her husband's magic boots, she almost fainted away. But little Tom Thumb pretended not to notice her white face. "I have come from your husband, ma'am," he said, smiling cheerfully. "These boots are proof of that. He has been taken prisoner and needs his bags of gold to buy his freedom. He gave me his boots so that I could come to you quickly."

The ogre's wife was so upset at the thought of losing her husband as well as her daughters that she did not stop to ask herself how he had been taken prisoner when before no one had dared even to speak to him. She gave Tom the bags of gold that were hidden under the floorboards and begged him to return quickly with news of her husband.

Tom made straight for his father's cottage and was there more quickly than you and I can say "cock robin." What a welcome he got and what praise his brothers gave him as they told all over again how he had saved them from the wicked ogre.

Then Tom Thumb threw the bags of gold on the table. "All our troubles are over," he cried. "This gold will make us rich for the rest of our lives."

Now those who know the woodcutter's family very well say that Tom Thumb gave the gold to the King for, as his mother said, it had most likely been stolen from the King and his subjects. Others say he took it back, in secret, to the ogre's wife and told her to hide it away for her old age.

Almost certainly Tom Thumb did not keep the gold after all, but then he had no need of it for the King made him the Court's Royal Messenger. Thanks to his magic boots, Tom Thumb was a great success in his new position. Soon he was given the title of Baron and a hundred gold pieces which he gave to his father.

In time, Tom Thumb became such a favorite at Court that the King invited him to live in his palace. Tom Thumb agreed, but he never grew too proud for his family, whom he visited every week so that he could see for himself they had everything they needed.

The Emperor's New Clothes

THERE WAS once an Emperor who loved new clothes more than he loved anything else in his empire. His greatest delight was to order gorgeous new robes at least three times a week. He spent all his money on his clothes and cared nothing for his soldiers or for the theater or dancing.

Now the great city where this Emperor lived was always crowded with strangers and many came hoping to see the Emperor wearing something new and very splendid and, of course, they were never disappointed.

One day two rogues came to the city and it wasn't long before they saw a way to cheat the Emperor and win for themselves a great deal of money. "Let's pretend we are weavers," one said to the other. "We'll go to the palace and tell the Emperor that we are the world's best weavers. We'll say the cloth we can weave is the finest ever seen."

The Emperor believed every word the two rogues said when, at last, they stood before him. "Give us gold and silk threads, your Majesty," said they, "and we will set up two looms here in the palace. We promise that you will have a cloth so wonderful that it will dazzle all eyes."

"Certainly, certainly I will!" cried the Emperor. "You will have everything you need to weave this wonderful cloth."

"There is just one thing, your Majesty," said one of the false weavers, bowing low. "Only those who are clever and worthy of their high office can see our cloth."

"Remarkable!" exclaimed the Emperor. "That makes the stuff even more interesting and wonderful!"

The next day the two cheats came to the palace. They brought with them two looms and they set these up in a room especially made ready for them. At their request they were given great quantities of golden thread and the finest colored silks. They were also given bags of gold to encourage them to work fast.

The Emperor was so excited about this wonderful cloth that he told everyone in the palace about it and how it could only be seen by those who were clever and worthy of the position they held at court. And it wasn't long before all the people in the city knew about the cloth and how only the very stupid would fail to see it.

By the end of the first week the Emperor felt he must know how the two weavers were getting on. "I won't go myself," he thought. "I will send my oldest and most trusted Minister. He is so clever that he will see the cloth and be able to tell me how beautiful it is."

Now the old Minister had served the Emperor for a very long time and he was very proud to be chosen. "I will give you a careful report," he told the Emperor before he hurried off to the weavers.

Imagine his surprise and horror when he entered the room where the two rogues sat at their looms pretending to work, and saw nothing . . . Absolutely nothing did he see, not even the smallest piece of cloth on the looms. "Gracious me!" thought the old man. "I can't see a thing." But he dared not say so. Instead, he fixed his spectacles more firmly on his nose and nodded once or twice.

Then one of the rogues said, "The colors and pattern are very fine. You agree, of course!"

And the other said, "Don't you think the Emperor will be pleased? The colors we have chosen will match his eyes!"

The old man was silent for a moment, staring at the empty looms. Then he said, "Yes, yes, very fine. I will tell the Emperor that the cloth you are weaving is truly beautiful."

The two false weavers then began to explain how they had made up the pattern and they told the Minister how much gold thread they had used. "We shall need more gold and more colored silks," they said at last. "Will you tell the Emperor?"

"I will indeed," said the old Minister, not daring to meet the rogues' eyes in case they should guess his secret.

The Emperor was delighted with his Minister's report. He sent more gold thread and silks to the weavers, which they hid away in a big sack as soon as it arrived.

At the end of the second week the Emperor said that he would go in person to the weavers' room to see if the cloth was nearly finished. He took with him several of his most trusted counselors and one or two other members of court who were known for their clever, witty remarks.

The two cheats got up from their empty looms and bowed low as the Emperor and his followers crowded into the room.

"Tell us, your Majesty, what you think," said one. "Are you not surprised at the beauty of the cloth and dazzled by the brilliant colors we have chosen?"

"What's this?" the Emperor thought, staring at the looms. "I can see nothing at all! Am I then so stupid? This is terrible. If I speak my thoughts people will say I am not fit to be their Emperor." So he said, "Yes, yes, it is very pretty, quite beautiful."

And all his Ministers repeated, "Yes, yes, quite beautiful." For they, like the Emperor, could not bring themselves to speak the truth.

The next day, one of the youngest Ministers spoke to the Emperor. "In two days, the great procession will take place when your Majesty

will walk through the city streets. Will you ask the weavers to finish the cloth and make it into a suit which you can wear in the great procession? The people want to see this wonderful cloth for themselves.''

"That is exactly what I intend to do," said the Emperor. And he sent two more bags of gold to the false weavers with a message, saying that they must work through the night to finish the cloth.

The weavers lit tall candles in their room so that the servants would report to the Emperor that they were indeed working all through the night. And, in the morning, they said the cloth was finished.

The Emperor himself hurried to the room when he was given the news and the cheats pretended to take the cloth from the loom. Then one rogue took up a big pair of scissors and pretended to be cutting the cloth while the other measured the Emperor and respectfully asked him how long he would like the train to be.

When the fitting was over, the rogues promised that the suit would be ready the next morning . . . the day of the great procession.

The Emperor rose early and made his way to the weavers' room. Behind him, came two servants carrying a long mirror.

The rogues greeted him with deep bows and respectfully asked him to take off his clothes so that he might be fitted with his new robes. The Emperor did so, and one rogue held his empty hands in the air, exclaiming, "Here are your trousers, your Majesty. They are as light as a spider's cobweb."

And the second rogue exclaimed, "And here is the jacket. Are not the colors dazzling?" And he, too, held up empty hands.

The two false weavers then pretended to help the Emperor into his new clothes and the Ministers, who had followed the Emperor into the room, all cried, "Oh, how wonderful they are, your Majesty! How they flatter you! What a perfect fit! What colors!"

The Emperor stared at himself in the long mirror. His eyes told him that he had nothing on but he did not dare say this. Instead, he said, "Yes, yes, they are a splendid fit. Very fine!" And turning to the two cheats, he said, "I will reward you with the title Imperial Court Weavers and see that you have more gold before the procession leaves the palace."

Then his oldest and most trusted Minister, who was in charge of the great procession, said, "The crowds have gathered in the streets, your Majesty, the musicians are in their places and all is ready."

Two chamberlains were appointed to hold the Emperor's long train and they stooped down and pretended to pick it up. And the Emperor left the palace and walked down the steps into the street.

"How splendid our Emperor looks today!" the crowd began to shout. "Bravo! What gorgeous clothes! What colors!" No one dared to speak the truth as the Emperor, under the rich canopy, walked slowly by.

Then, suddenly, a little boy cried, "But he has nothing on! Our Emperor is not wearing any clothes at all!"

His father tried to hush his little son but the words had been heard. More children began to shout and laugh. "Nothing on! The Emperor has nothing on!"

Soon all the people took up the cry and many began to laugh. The Emperor heard what they said. Suddenly, he knew that what his people said was true. And, oh, how sad he was and how ashamed! Clearly he had been tricked and cheated by the weavers. But it was his love for new clothes that had turned him into a fool. Still, he was the Emperor. He could not leave the great procession. He must walk through the streets as if nothing was wrong. So the Emperor walked on and behind him came the two chamberlains pretending to carry a train that wasn't there!

The Emperor was never again so fond of new clothes for he had learned his lesson. But it will be a long time before the people of that great city forget the day of the great procession. And if you are wonder-

ing about the two rogues; why, long before the procession was over, they were galloping their horses out of the city, their bags stuffed with enough gold to last them all the days of their lives.